SILVER BERRIES
AND
CHRISTMAS MAGIC

by Urslan Judith Gaffington

illustrated by Steven Morris

jacket & interior design by Steven Morris

RiverMoon Books
PO Box 532
Stony Brook, NY 11790-0532
Manufactured in Singapore
First Edition, 1996
to mykerrybaby

Publisher's Cataloguing in Publication
(Prepared by Quality Books, Inc.)
Gaffington, Urslan
Silver berries and Christmas magic/ by Urslan Gaffington;
illustrations by Steven Morris
p. cm.
SUMMARY: The story of Tiemma Claus (Santa's wife), who helps
Santa reach all the children on Christmas Eve.
ISBN 0-9647811-0-7
1. Christmas—Juvenile fiction. I. Title
PZ7.G3445Sil 1996 [Fic]
QBI95-2063

"**B**IRD BOOTS! the squirrels!" Leddy cried, suddenly coming wide awake. She had been so tired from playing in the snow all day that she had gone to bed without feeding them.

She jumped out of bed and yanked on her coat and boots. As quietly as falling snow, Leddy tiptoed past her parents' bedroom then hurried to the kitchen. Grabbing a handful of peanuts, she raced out the door and ran down the icy steps. All of a sudden she was laying face down in the snow with peanuts scattered everywhere.

"Bird boots, that's cold," she grumbled, lifting her face up.

"Do birds really wear boots around here?"

Startled, Leddy pushed herself up, brushed the snow from her eyes, and looked around. There in the snow, munching on the squirrels' peanuts, were two — well, she didn't know what they were. So she asked, "What are you?"

"*What* are we?" The one who had spoken lifted his chin proudly. "Why, we're well-mannered, honest, intelligent, very tired — "

"Oh, just tell her we're Snow Fairies!" the other, smaller creature blurted out.

"Okay. Okay." He started over. "I'm Kels." He pointed to his friend. "She's Jaxx. And we're Snow Fairies."

"Bird boots!" Leddy repeated, rubbing her eyes, thinking she must be dreaming. She'd never heard of Snow Fairies.

"She said it again, Jaxx." Kels looked around. "I don't see any birds wearing boots."

"*Forget* the bird boots, Kels," Jaxx snapped. "We need help."

Still startled, and now a little embarrassed, Leddy silently promised to stop saying 'bird boots' so often. But staring at the Snow Fairies, she shook her head and immediately broke her promise. *Bird boots*, they couldn't be real! Then, just as she was thinking they couldn't be real, they moved.

"*Wings!*" she cried, staring at them. "You have wings!"

"Of course we have wings," Kels said, shocked that anyone would think they didn't. "All Snow Fairies have wings."

Since Leddy had never seen a Snow Fairy she figured she ought to believe them.

"Be nice, Kels, would you? Maybe she'll help us."

"What's wrong?" Leddy asked.

Kels began. "Well, you see, little girl — "

"My name's Leddy."

"Right. Now, as I was saying, little girl — I mean Leddy. You see, there was this big, really big, really, really big — "

"Snow storm," an exasperated Jaxx cut in. She turned to Leddy. "He'll go on like that until birds *do* wear boots. He tore his wing and can't fly. We have to fix it so we can get back to the North Pole."

"The North Pole! You mean where Santa lives?" Leddy was back to thinking she must be dreaming. "But I thought elves lived with Santa."

"They do," Kels said. "Winterland Elves are the best toymakers in the world. But we live there, too."

Leddy frowned. "The North Pole's very far away. How did you get here?"

"We rode in on the storm," Kels said simply.

"We're the best wind riders," Jaxx said proudly. "Better than - well, just about anyone."

"That sounds like fun," Leddy said, wishing she had wings and could ride the wind.

Kels looked at his torn wing. "Usually it is."

"Do you think you can help?" Jaxx asked hopefully.

"I'll try." Leddy's parents had taught her if she tried hard enough she could figure out the answer to almost any problem, no matter how big. Leddy figured a Snow Fairy's torn wing was a big problem. She studied Kels' wing. "What we need is a patch."

"And some magic," Jaxx added.

"But there's no magic around here," Leddy said.

"Tee says there's magic everywhere, in everything. Right, Kels?"

"Yup. Emma says you just have to know how to look."

Leddy looked around. "But all I see is snow and trees."

"Then snow and trees it is."

Jaxx took Kels' hand and together the two Snow Fairies spoke into the night.

"Snow and trees, snow and trees,
aren't we lucky to have toes and knees.
Snow and trees, snow and trees,
we have a problem, won't you help us please?"

No sooner had they finished speaking, then a gust of wind whipped up. It swirled about the treetops, tugging at the branches until it loosened a solitary brown leaf. The leaf tumbled down, brushing Leddy's shoulder before it settled on the snowy ground between the two fairies.

"There's a bit of Emma's magic for you." Kels placed the leaf in Leddy's hand. "What do you think we should do with this?"

Leddy studied it for a moment. "It can be the patch!"

Jaxx smiled. "Now all we need is something sticky to hold it on with."

"We don't need magic for that." Leddy waved. "Come on, I know what we can use."

She led the way into her warm kitchen. While Leddy got a jar of honey from the cabinet, Jaxx flew onto the counter and Kels scrambled onto the table.

"Are Tee and Emma Snow Fairies, too?" Leddy asked as she began to patch Kels' wing with the leaf and honey. "Or are they elves?"

Kels laughed. "No, no, no. You see, I usually call her Emma, and Jaxx always calls her Tee, but her name is Tiemma. Tiemma Claus."

"Tiemma *Claus*?" Leddy repeated.

"Yeah. You know, Santa's wife."

Leddy put up her hands. "Wait! Wait! Wait! Snow Fairies, magic, Tiemma Claus. Bird boots! there's a lot I don't know about the North Pole."

Kels twisted his head around. "Are you finished with my wing?" When Leddy nodded, Kels smiled and poked his head into the cookie jar. He pulled out a cookie and sat back. "Where were we? Oh, right. You said there was a lot you didn't know about the North Pole. Well, Leddy, what do you want to know?"

"Wait," Jaxx cut in. "It's really late. Leddy should be in bed. Sleeping."

"Oh, but I can't sleep now!" Leddy cried. "I want to hear about Tiemma and her magic and — and — and everything."

"Jaxx is right, Leddy," Kels said, shaking his head.

"Just one story? Please. Then I'll go right to sleep."

"You promise?"

"I promise, Jaxx."

Jaxx looked from Leddy to Kels then back to Leddy. "All right. But only one."

"Great!" Leddy exclaimed at the same time Kels said sadly, "Only one?"

★

Knowing how much Kels liked to tell stories, Jaxx repeated, "Only one."

"Well then it's got to be a good one. Hmmm." Kels rubbed his chin as he thought a moment. "Okay, okay. I got it!" He took a bite from the cookie. "There's a story that has been told down through the years by elves and fairies about a time long, long, long ago. Way, way before, even before — "

Jaxx nudged Leddy. "Birds *will* be wearing boots before he gets to the story."

Leddy giggled as Kels sighed. "Okay. It was a cold and snowy Christmas Eve. Santa was very, very late and Tiemma was upset. The fairies and elves knew she was because she hadn't taken one sip of her pumpkin cider - not one single sip. That's her favorite, you know?"

Leddy shook her head. She hadn't known.

Jaxx nodded. "Oh yeah. Tiemma *loves* pumpkin cider."

"As I was saying," Kels continued, "she was fidgeting with the snowflake necklace Santa had given her long ago. She always does that when she's worried. You see, he gave it to her when — "

Jaxx sighed. *"One* story, Kels."

"Oh, right. When Santa finally got home, he was very, very, very tired."

"The problem," Jaxx explained, "was that every year there were more and more children. Santa needed a way to go faster or he wouldn't be able to reach all the children next Christmas Eve."

"Right." Kels took another bite of his cookie. "So, over the next couple of months everyone at the North Pole tried to think of a way to help Santa. But it wasn't until a Monday — "

"It was a Tuesday, Kels," Jaxx reminded him.

"Okay, it was a Tuesday morning — "

"It was afternoon," Jaxx corrected helpfully.

"Oh, yeah, it was," Kels agreed.

"You see, Leddy," Jaxx said, "there was going to be a party for three Winterland Elves who had earned their *Totally Magnificent Toymaker Certificates.*"

Licking the honey off her fingers, Leddy sat in her warm kitchen and listened while Jaxx, with a little help from Kels, told the tale of Tiemma and the silver berries.

SANTA AND TIEMMA were working in their cozy kitchen. Santa was busy making sweet muddleberry mush and brown sugar dumplings which Winterland Elves loved more than anything - except Christmas Eve.

Tiemma was mixing up her favorite pumpkin cider. As often happened, the tip of her long silver-white braid ended up in the kettle. When she turned and reached for a bottle of her special spice, her braid flipped out.

"Tiemma, your hair," Santa chuckled, watching cider drip from her braid onto the chair and floor.

"Ohh, not again," Tiemma groaned. "I don't have time for this." She looked at the rag that hung beside the cupboard across the room. Smiling, she said,

"We've made the mush, we've made the pies.
I'm in a rush, it's no surprise.
My hands are full, I've much to do.
Time is short, I wish you flew."

Instantly Tiemma's fingertips began to tickle and tingle with the feel of magic. The rag lifted off the hook into the air.

Working magic also made her kneecaps itch, so scratching her knees against the table leg, she continued,

"Silly blue rag, just floating on air,
please clean up the mess, on the floor and the chair."

Quick as a shooting star, the blue rag zipped over the chair and floor, leaving not a drop of cider anywhere, then settled back down on its hook.

Amused, Santa chuckled as he carried food out of the kitchen. Tiemma however was left wondering if her magic could somehow help Santa get to all the children on Christmas Eve.

Later that night, while the rest of the North Pole slept peacefully, Tiemma tossed and turned. She kept thinking about Santa and the children. When she finally fell asleep she dreamt of Santa trudging through the snow, his sack of toys slung over his shoulder, the blue rag circling his head, and reindeer running through the clouds above him. It was a very strange dream indeed!

The next day, Tiemma noticed reindeer more than she ever had before. It seemed they were everywhere. She even thought she saw them with their noses pressed against her kitchen window watching her bake gingerbread cookies. And when she took her gingerbread men from the oven, they weren't shaped like men at all but like reindeer!

Tiemma was so startled she dropped the pan. Reindeer cookies fell to the floor. Immediately, she set her magic to the mess.

> *"**H**ot and gingery cookies galore,*
> *up quick and clean, up off the floor."*

The reindeer cookies flew off the floor back onto the pan, and the pan settled onto the table.

"Oh, my!" Tiemma exclaimed. "That's *got* to be it! I can't wait to tell everyone!"

"Reindeer fly! Impossible! Ridiculous!" scoffed one of the elves who had gathered with Santa and the fairies to hear Tiemma's idea.

"And I'll ride this flying reindeer while I carry my sack?" Santa asked, liking the idea very much. Until another one came into his mind. "Or maybe a little sleigh for the flying reindeer to pull?"

"Think of *all* those children," Tiemma said. "And *all* those toys."

Stroking his beard, his brow crinkled in thought, he nodded. "A very large sleigh with lots of reindeer."

"Reindeer fly! Impossible! Ridiculous!" the first elf huffed, still not convinced.

"But Tiemma," one of the smaller elves cut in. "Even if you do make the reindeer fly, there's still the problem of the chimneys."

"Sometimes there aren't any," said another elf.

"And sometimes they're just too small," said another still.

"I hadn't forgotten," Tiemma said. "I'll work on that, too."

"Then you'll need magic more powerful than any you've made before," the second elf said.

"Reindeer fly! Impossible! Ridiculous!" the first elf said once again.

A fairy flew up to him. "Remember when Tiemma suggested tying iron blades onto our boot bottoms and gliding on the frozen pond? You thought we shouldn't even try." The fairy tapped his finger on his lips. "Weren't you the one who never wanted to stop?"

The elf blushed. "That *was* a lot of fun."

"Sometimes," Tiemma said, "ideas sound impossible before they are tried."

"So, what do you say?" the fairy asked.

"Reindeer fly!" the elf snapped grumpily. Then he laughed. "Of course! Why not!"

"It's settled," Santa said excitedly. "Tiemma, while you and the fairies work on your magic, the elves and I will build the sleigh and pick the reindeer."

⚜

From that day on, Tiemma spent most of her time with the fairies gathering the ingredients for her magic - much of it from secret places only a fairy could find. Into the special pouch she always wore, Tiemma tossed some of this and some of that, and mixed a little bit more of this with a little bit less of that until she had a combination she thought would work.

When she was ready to test it on Santa and his reindeer she called out a warning. But that wasn't necessary. As soon as the elves saw her scratching her knees, they knew she was working her magic and started to run. Laughing, they scurried here and there, bumping into each other, falling over things trying to get out of the way since they never knew where Santa would land.

Over the next several weeks, Santa and his reindeer were flipped over, flung about, and tossed more times than a platter of pancakes. They plowed into snowdrifts so often Santa's beard and mustache grew icicles. Each time the elves helped him up, Santa dusted himself off and laughed so merrily his "Ho-Ho-Ho" echoed through the village. When Tiemma discovered some of the North Polers had bet lingleberry tarts on how many times she would flip Santa, she chuckled. And bet three herself.

Not a day went by that the fairies didn't bring Tiemma something she could add to her magic. But no matter how many different combinations and amounts she used, Santa, his sleigh, and reindeer just couldn't fly.

Something was missing.

As Christmas Eve approached, Tiemma grew more and more worried. She needed to think, and she always did her best thinking while walking through the snow-filled forest. With a basket of food to feed to the animals, Tiemma headed for the forest and a thinking walk. In no time at all her basket was empty, yet she was no closer to an answer than when she began.

Suddenly a beam of sunlight broke through the thick tops of the forest trees and bounced off a cluster of icicles. It made a brilliant arrow of golden light that disappeared into a large group of trees just ahead of her. Tiemma stopped and slowly looked around. Everything was new. She had been so caught up in her worries, she had walked deeper into the forest than ever before.

Intrigued, Tiemma followed the golden trail through the trees. It led to a small bush that twinkled and glistened. As she moved closer she realized that what sparkled were actually tiny, shimmering, silver berries. She gasped. All her life, she had heard about the bush whose silver berries grew and ripened when the children of the world were brave or honest or when they did a kindness or tried their very best. She had always believed that, *that* magic, the magic of children, was truly the most powerful magic in the world.

With each step her worries faded away. By the time she reached out to touch a silver berry Tiemma knew she had found the missing ingredient for her magic.

She had found the magic of children.

On her way home, with a handful of silver berries glowing in her pouch, Tiemma thought about when to use them. The Winter Solstice marked the beginning of the most magical and busy time of year for all who lived at the North Pole. That night they always had a grand celebration. If her new magic worked, and she believed in her heart it would, two nights from now there would be even more to celebrate!

On the night of the Winter Solstice giant bonfires leapt towards the sky lighting up the village square. Snowflakes dotted the heads of the North Polers and the delicious smell of roasted corn and spiced nuts tickled their noses as they arrived at the celebration.

Throughout the evening, the clapping of hands and the tapping of toes mingled with the snapping and popping of the bonfires as dancers swirled and twirled to merry songs.

Later, when the sky filled with midnight stars, and all the food was eaten, all the songs were sung, and all the dances were danced, Tiemma whispered to Santa, "It's time."

Hand-in-hand, Tiemma and Santa led the reindeer and sleigh through the crowd. As they walked past the bonfires, Tiemma said,

"We're here to
join the spirit
of the children
of the Earth,
to the jolly
happy traveler
who fills this
night with mirth."

Santa stepped into his sleigh and took up his reins. Tiemma reached into her pouch and grasped a handful of magic.

"We are made of
many things,
friendships true,
mighty dreams.
Of stars and suns
and moons lit bright,
mixed and matched
and stirred just right."

Fingertips tingling and kneecaps itching, Tiemma tossed her magic high into the air. Brilliant bursts of silver-white light sparkling with red and green floated through the night sky and settled over Santa, his sleigh and eight reindeer.

Tiemma nodded to Santa. The elves and fairies held their breaths as Santa gave the reins a snap.

The reindeer started to walk. Then to prance. Then they flew. Up and up. Higher and higher. A loud cheer rang out as Santa and his reindeer flew around the North Pole sky.

Everyone grew quiet when it was time for Santa to land. Which he did — gently — with no sound except his laughter.

After the rest of the North Polers had left for their beds, Santa and Tiemma sat on a fallen tree.

"It worked," Santa said softly. "Your magic worked."

"With help from the magic of children," Tiemma said.

Santa turned to his wife, his face alight with wonder and awe. "It was amazing to soar over the night clouds and to zoom past the stars. I'm sure I'll be able to reach all the children now. It's going to be a wonderful Christmas."

On Christmas Eve all that remained were the last minute chores.

While the elves and fairies packed the sleigh and fed the reindeer, Tiemma studied the weather information, seeking the best route around the world, then discussed it with Santa as he checked his list one final time.

When the sun had set and evening had arrived, Tiemma dressed in her beautiful red gown and braided holly and ribbons into her hair. Santa put on his red velvet suit and combed his beard and mustache. Then Tiemma grabbed up her velvet cloak and Santa his red and white hat, and out the door and into the night they went.

In the village square all the North Polers gathered around Santa's sleigh to wave good-bye.

"Just touch here," Tiemma said, kissing Santa on his nose. "And chimneys won't be a problem."

Santa scrunched up his face. "It tingles."

"Of course," Tiemma said as he settled into his sleigh, "it's magic."

At last it was time for Santa to leave. Tiemma, the fairies and elves all cheered as the reindeer leapt forward, climbed into the night sky, and flew out of sight.

Back home Tiemma sat in her chair by the fire contentedly drinking pumpkin cider and eating gingerbread. She was pleased in the part she had played that Christmas. Now Santa would do the rest, bringing his special happiness and joy to the children of the world - each and every one of them.

Before she knew it, the front door flew open.

A gloriously happy, wind blown Santa tossed aside his empty sack and held out his hand. "Come with me, Tiemma. We'll glide down a moonbeam and race a shooting star."

Her eyes twinkling with happiness, Tiemma took Santa's hand. Laughing, they ran out to the sleigh.

"Pick a cloud, Tiemma, and hold on."

ND that's the way it's been ever since," Kels said, still munching on a cookie. "And always will be as long as children try their very best. "

" And are honest and brave," Jaxx added from her seat on the counter in Leddy's kitchen.

"And remember to act with kindness," Kels continued, "there will always be silver berries."

"Oh, bird boots," Leddy cried. "I get it now. It's us kids! As long as we make silver berries, Tiemma will make the magic and Santa's reindeer will fly."

"Talk about flying," Jaxx said, "it's time for us to go."

"Thanks for the help, Leddy." Kels started to stand, then sat back down. "You know, you really should hear the story about — "

"Kels!" Jaxx rolled her eyes. "We have to go. *Now!*"

Leddy's sleepy giggle turned into a wide yawn. Closing her eyes, she laid her head on the table. The fairies gently touched her shoulder and whispered their promise to return. Then, with a flutter of fairy wings, they were gone, and Leddy was alone.

Except for her dreams of Snow Fairies, silver berries, and Tiemma's Christmas magic.